THE SUBSTANCE OF THINGS HOPED FOR

a journey to find faith amid the perils of pride

Jeffery T. Morton

TATE PUBLISHING, LLC

Published in the United States of America
by Tate Publishing, LLC
127 East Trade Center Terrace
Mustang, OK 73064
(888) 361–9473

This novel is a work of fiction. Names, descriptions, entities and incidents included in the story are products of the author's imagination. Any resemblance to actual persons, events and entities is entirely coincidental.

ISBN: 1–9332900–7-2

DEDICATION

For my lovely daughter, Heather.
May this help you keep the fires of Faith burning bright in
the years to come.

ACKNOWLEDGEMENTS

A special thank you to Tatyana for helping me find my way back to happiness, to Sandy for understanding my passion. To Jacques for being so supportive during the difficult times as well as the good. To Mary Jane who accepted that I spent every morning doing "something" before work, and never questioned why or what I was doing.

I also want to thank the pastors of my church who kept my faith alive and strong with their thought-provoking messages.

A thank you to the folks at Tate Publishing for taking a chance on an unknown writer.

And the greatest thanks and praise to God for showering me with many blessings, none of which do I take for granted, and for blessing me with the greatest gift of all—his son and eternal life.

INTRODUCTION

I began working on this poem about twelve years ago. Over those twelve years, the poem has changed a great deal and has evolved, as have I. When I began planning the outline of the poem, I was fresh out of college and (somewhat ironically) my desire to write was driven by my Pride. I had been a student of Classical British and Elizabethan literature, and wanted to produce something that would eventually become my legacy. I wanted to create something that would succeed me after I had passed away. I was not so grandiose to think I would become another Shakespeare or Milton (these great writers can be most humbling), but hoped to create something I could leave behind for my family in generations to come. To leave them with something that might help them understand the thoughts and beliefs I held.

In the beginning I struggled many a night over endless pads of paper, working diligently, trying to make it as complex and prosaic as the writers I had so adored. Since I wanted to emulate my favorite writers, such as John Milton, Christopher Marlowe, Andrew Marvell, Edmund Spenser, Sir Phillip Sydney, Geoffrey Chaucer, Dante, Edward Fitzgerald, Matthew Arnold, and John Langland, I chose a spiritual theme, and the common literary structure of the time—an enlightened journey. I must confess that at that time I was not especially a spiritual man, though I was raised in a family that encouraged belief in God. My intent was not really to convey some spiritual passion, or some great insights on Faith, or even to share my re-birth and re-awakening. It was, in truth, a rather grandiose venture to see if I could write as poetically as the ones I most admired so I might have a chance of being immortalized like them.

But, life happens. As time progressed, I was consumed with other things in my life: advancing in my career, buying a house, establishing a family, and raising a child. In light of all this, the poem was cast into the shadows, and was neglected for a long time; I was only able to spend little pieces of time to create a stanza or two, but the project seemed endless.

In time, I became so consumed with my worldly aspirations that I drifted further and further from the little faith that I still had from my youth. I drifted further from my writing, and drifted further from the foundations that helped me define right and wrong. I began to justify the sinful nature that was growing within me. I kept my sins silent and to myself, I rationalized them and fought alone with the guilt that remained.

When things seemed to be heading for disaster, a colleague came to lead me back. I was invited to church for

Thanksgiving service, and while I sat and listened to the pastor, the feelings that had long escaped me, the inner joy, the beautiful love, the awesome forgiveness overwhelmed me. I kept attending the church and eventually made a decision to stop all my sinful ways. But that would not be enough. I was moved by the spirit to not only change, but to also confess my sins to the ones that I loved. At that time I didn't understand why I should do this. They didn't know what I had been doing, and I was going to stop, so why would I want to hurt them by telling them what I had been doing? But now I understand. This confession, this disclosure created a transparency that strengthened my resolve to stay on the right path. Secrets enable sin and feed temptation.

Now, picture this, a young man who thinks, "I will do what God wants, I will do the right thing for once, and everything will be happy and blissful again." But this is not how it worked out. I confessed my sins, and told my family that I intended to change my ways now that I had reaffirmed my faith. My reward? I lost everything, my home, my friends, my wife, and precious time with my daughter. I lost the respect of my family, and I lost respect in myself. I moved into a small apartment, and lived by myself without anyone to help my through this troubled time except God. During this time, I read my Bible, prayed, and almost every night I cried.

For some strange reason, one of the very few things I brought with me when I left my home was my poem. I began reading it again, reading it with different eyes. I realized it was one thing to praise God and Faith when things are going well, and to say or write the words of what one should or should not do, but it is true faith that can still praise him when we are in the throes of sorrow and pain. I thought about Milton, and how he lost what was probably the most valuable thing to a writer—his eyesight. I thought about how, despite his loss, he still found his love for God to be so great that he wanted to praise him in some of the most remarkably written and amazing pieces of literature that have ever been written by man: *Paradise Lost, Paradise Regained,* and *Sampson Agonistes.* Now, my intent was not to become Milton, or to even be published, but my goal was to have a daily devotional time and way to express my love for God despite the trials and turmoil I was facing in my life.

I re-wrote the entire poem spending literally hours upon hours re-writing each line, each stanza, and each canto. I removed entire cantos, and transformed it from being a complex work with vague allusions to obscure literary references for the purpose of self-glorification, to a work that would hopefully glorify Him. Having said this, I should also tell you, the reader, that the poem was not stripped of *all* complexities. There are still a number of allegorical levels which must be considered, and a number of symbolic references, metaphors, and images throughout the poem that should be considered when it is read. But, to tell you more, would be a disservice.

I said my intent was not to publish, but as I shared my poem with friends, family, and co-workers with hopes that I might touch someone else's life, I realized that I should try to reach further than this small circle if at all possible. And now here it is. If I help one person through a difficult time, help one re-ignite their faith, or help one rediscover the bountiful and beautiful love that comes from our Father and his Son, then I will feel my efforts in creating this work will have been rewarded.

With Love in Christ,
Jeffery T. Morton
December 1st, 2004

A Journey Begins

In a vast meadow, in a bleak and dismal world,
I waded carelessly amongst a sea of grass;
Where tempestuous blades angrily swayed and swirled,
Much as my mind, with thoughts of things past.

The whispish white clouds, floated dangerously high,
While that matriarch star shone majestically bright;
Sitting like a queen in her court of Lapis sky,
Her place pre-defined—established by divine right.

Where blustering Spring winds chilled the Sun's heat,
And softened the strength of her warming glow,
On this annual occasion when the season's meet—
When the waters of Life begin again to flow.

I felt confused, felt my loyalties divided,
For I knew not where my hopes and heart belonged:
With Spring, when the fire of Life is ignited,
Or with peaceful Winter nights which were dark and long.

While the Winter winds numbed my nose and ears,
The Sun of Spring fought to comfort and keep me warm.
And though to Spring's life-giving power I was endeared,
The demise of Winter, I still didst sadly mourn.

Unable to escape the worries of my mind,
I prayed for someone to show me the way,
To reveal Truth, so inner peace I might find,
So my worries might be abolished and allayed.

For this was my Hope when I walked through that field:
That someone might come to help me understand,
Might come to explain the purpose of my ordeals,
Might come to enlighten me to the ways of man.

I wondered why the faith of my childhood disappeared,
Whether God did, in truth, have for me a plan,,
Whether my destiny could be altered or steered,
Or if my Fate was decided when my life began?

In my heart and mind, waves of questions endlessly rolled,
Like an ocean current it pulled me further out to sea,
Pulled me further into the depths of the unknown,
And caused me to question and doubt what I believe.

How can man have Faith in something he cannot see?
From what internal spring does his Hope and Faith flow?
How can he know what is Truth or what to believe,
When his world is filled with so many unknowns?

I allowed my thoughts to further drift and wander,
As I lay my head to rest upon the cool damp ground,
So many questions were there for me to ponder,
Questions, for which, no answers have e'er been found.

I awoke, startled and stirred by some peaceful presence,
And jumped promptly to my feet, eager to arise,
And saw to the East, a soft and shadowy essence,
That stood hilltop and blended with the midday skies.

As he crossed the meadow, and drew closer to me,
I saw that he seemed to float rather than walk,
Like some mystical ethereal spirit, ghost, or being,
That could effortlessly pass through trees and rocks.

As he stood before me, in the sun of mid-day,
I could finally see his face, his size and shape:
His light auburn hair, that upon his shoulders lay,
His ruddy cheeks, and his innocent boyish face.

Clothed like one who was from another time or place,
He wore a gown of sackcloth, that was tattered and torn,
With a rope of red, white and gold tied about his waist,
And sandals that were well-weathered and well-worn.

From his pale face, his youthful eyes glistened,
Shone with an undaunted Hope of tomorrow,
Gleamed with youthful innocence and ambition—
But, also spoke of a silent inner sorrow.

"Follow me," he said, "to a place that is ageless,
Where men have been trapped by the wiles of Pride,
Where men create their own prisons—their own cages,
Where men have been condemned by their own lies."

"Come and follow me." He beckoned effortlessly,
"Through yonder meadows to witness their doom,
To learn how Pride can determine our destiny,
To see those forever trapped within Pride's tomb."

The Sun was set high in that clear and cloudless sky,
While those mischievous Brothers blew their gusty airs,
Danced with the treetops, whispered their secrets and
sighed,
And watched the Fates weave, snarl and cut without care.

As I followed him, I behind and he afore,
I strained to see what lie ahead—to learn from my eyes.
And while we walked, he told of his travels before:
His visits to Purgatory, to Hell, and to Paradise.

He said Faith could always guide and lead the way,
Could deliver me from the world's lies and deceits,
Could reveal Truth, could bring order to disarray,
And could untangle the webs of Pride and Disbelief.

We labored forth, and came to a spacious clearing,
Where he stopped and stared deep into my puzzled eyes.
"There are many Truths you are afraid of hearing,
But ignorance can never make a man more wise."

"An open heart and mind is required to grow,
For Faith to be truly understood and received.
For Life without Faith, is Life without true Love and Hope,
Is a Life without joy—is a Life without inner peace."

"Many have searched in vain to find what all men seek:
That elusive path to eternal happiness,
That one 'thing' which will make their lives complete,
That which will fill the void, and abolish emptiness."

"But be wary of Pride—do not let her lead your life,
For she will cause you to follow the world's ways,
Will cause you to doubt what your heart knows is right,
Cause you to follow lost sheep, and the shepherd betray."

"Beware of Envy and of Pride's many dangers,
They will stunt and impede your spiritual growth,
Shall suppress your will, will breed resentment and anger."
And so it was, with wizened words, that this child spoke.

He seemed to speak without judgment, more like a friend,
Who projected the warmth of love in his presence—
A warmth that was unceasing and without end;
A warmth that glowed from his youth and innocence

I asked, "How does man's Pride grow? Where is it born?
Does it lay quietly dormant within our very souls,
Silently asleep until the fear of Fate is born,
Until destiny is recognized and mortality is known?"

"Is Pride born from the desire to be remembered?
The desperate Hope of being immortalized?
Does man really think legacies can live forever,
Or that he can avoid the deadly grasp of Time?"

"So many questions!" He said smiling to me.
"First, friend, you must learn to understand yourself,
To see through the many self-deceits and lies,
To see the senselessness of worldly fame and wealth."

"Pride's large and ornate house is filled with hate,
With halls that weave and wind through many rooms.
She misguides man and redefines his destiny and fate,
And then traps him forever within her Hellish tomb."

"For many, what was their symbol of distinction,
What once made them feel powerful and great,
Has become the cause of their pain and perdition,
Is now the source of their eternal suffering state."

"You will soon see those who are lost and hopeless,
But, like Lazarus, you cannot soothe their pain,
It will be like trying to give sight to the lifeless,
For how they are now, is how they must remain."

"Come, we must travel while we have the Sun,
For Night's veil will soon enshroud the skies,
The brightness of day will be lost and undone,
And darkness will come to blur our weary eyes."

A Room Divided

After we walked through meadows gold and green,
We stopped to peer down into a valley below,
Where a white and marble hall could be seen.

The columns, which were white like freshly fallen snow,
Were each crowned with a most elegant cornice,
And stood like disciplined soldiers in perfect rows.

As those magnificent columns towered above us,
I saw each possessed such a pure and glassy sheen,
That they reflected the sun's great brightness.

Never before had I ever beheld or ever seen,
Such a blinding light,such an illumination,
As did come from that place that seemed so pure and clean.

"Beware," my guide spoke with quiet consternation,
"Beware of this place of the Prideful and Zealous,
Of the polished lies, the dark deceits, and the self-fascina-
tion."

"Although your senses may be consumed and enveloped,
It is a reflection, a false light, that it does emit—
One that distorts Truth, and leaves Reason undeveloped."

Upon the stairs, I saw a beautiful woman didst sit.
She peered at her lap lonesomely, her face I could not see,
But her beauty, with this place, didst seem to fit.

More than she, who from Phoebus didst frantically flee,
I thought this woman didst more lovely seem,
As we neared and left the shelter of a Laurel tree.

As we drew closer, she arose to greet us like a queen,
But, as we began to ascend those glassy stairs,
I saw in her eyes a sorrow I ne'er before had seen:

Her cheeks were sallow beneath her mussed and matted hair,
And her red and sunken eyes seemed wild and disturbed;
This I witnessed as we drew closer to her unprotected lair.

"Pursue glory while you may . . ." she softly whispered,
As though reciting some special spell or incantation,
"Live for death comes, live so you might be remembered."

As she prattled on, without ceasing or hesitation,
Her eyes remained downcast and fixed upon the ground,
And she never once moved from her assigned station.

Without delay, the marble stairs we didst mount,
And then traveled on silently and without hurry,
Into a darkness which did us embrace and surround.

With Him guiding me, I felt at ease and without worry,
As we traveled through tunnels damp, dark and unclean;
Traveled through corridors that were stark, gray and dreary.

Soon, I heard a noise, distant and faint as in a dream,
The sound of a thousand far-off voices echoing,
Rumbling and murmuring like some shallow stream.

Unsure of what lie ahead, I followed without knowing,
I followed with Faith, and never let Him leave my sight,
Until that gray hall came to a bright and wide opening.

When we entered into that place of brighter light,
I could see a multitude of men arguing ardently,
Screaming angrily and engaged in ruthless fight.

Never before had I seen such chaos and insanity,
So I watched and stayed safely within the threshold,
And witnessed all with disbelief and solemnity.

A crack in the floor, which bred a mossy green mold,
Zig-zagged and separated them into clusters and clans—
By Religion, by skin-color, by young and by old.

As I watched, I saw one youth lunge at an older man.
His intense anger had caused him to trip over the line,
Where he instantly aged, and now couldst barely stand.

As he now allied himself 'gainst his former side,
I thought of those who did not their father heed;
Of Icarus, who haplessly flew into those fateful skies.

Of that prodigal son who wanted to be free,
Who thought he was wise enough to find his own way,
And nearly allowed his Pride, to define his destiny.

But, despite his ways, his father's love did not fade.
And when that young man fell into peril and poverty,
His father was there to give love and to save.

"We believe in ourselves" the youth cried confidently,
"We don't need anyone to guide us or show us the way,
We will succeed relying on our own abilities!"

"You will surely fail!" I heard the older men say,
"Without us, you will only suffer endlessly,
And your ignorance will be your end someday!"

The other groups argued just as bitterly.
Saying the others were evil and could not be trusted,
That they were ignorant, slothful, and untrustworthy.

I saw how Pride interfered, as she always must,
How she can turn a man from the ones that love him,
And can make a tongue so sharp it never dulls or rusts.

For they who reside in Pride's false kingdom,
Become captive and fettered by Pride's great weight—
They forget love's power, and abandon true Reason.

I watched as the men, grew more bitter and more irate,
Spoke louder and louder, unrestrained and undeterred;
Hoping someone would listen to the words they did state.

Becoming frustrated with not being heeded or heard,
Many would lunge at their opponents in desperation—
While others would only hurl insults and hurtful words.

Some even stood like statues making proclamations;
But no one learned, and nothing was truly being taught,
Except how to embrace anger, hate, and frustration.

And so it was that Pride kept them captive and apart,
Trapped by their own bitterness and their endless war.
Then my guide broke the silence, and began to talk:

"They will continue this battle forever more.
For their Pride will only grow, and shall never die,
As long as Forgiveness is forgotten, and love is ignored."

Through the crowd, an elderly man did us find,
And hobbled to us with a crooked cane in hand;
His face seemed most gentle, wizened and kind.

He spoke, when he finally did before us stand:
"What is this I see? What do mine eyes behold?
But two un-allied, two without a place to stand."

As his quizzical and condensed face did unfold,
I followed to where his crooked finger led—
To that fateful fissure, to that divisive line of mold.

I saw that I had not chosen my place among these men.
"Come, you must define yourself . . . you must select!
Come, and choose a group!" He impatiently said.

I replied, "For each, and all I have respect.
And I strive for my love to reign over my Pride,
So, no loyalties will I declare, none will I reject."

The man grumbled and then abruptly left our side,
And returned to his fellows on the elderly team,
Where he quickly blended with them and didst hide.

"If they allow themselves to be guided by Pride,
It will only grow stronger, like some insidious disease,
That consumes its host—its very spirit and its mind."

Then, from my threshold station I was released,
And between the many factions the room we crossed.
And when we passed, their fighting briefly ceased.

But, sadly, I knew Hope for them was past—was lost.

The Travelers

As we walked along a cold cobbled path,
My young guide and I strode side by side,
And as we walked, he told me tales of people past.

He spoke of those who could not resist Pride,
Who were unable to feel complete and whole,
Who were unable to find peace in this earthly life.

"What treasures doth your heart dearly hold?
Does it seek, symbols of success and worldly images?
Beware, for where your heart lies, there also lies your soul."

"There were four men, returning from a pilgrimage,
Who gathered 'bout a fire when had set the sun,
Together seeking comfort, warmth, and courage."

"The first was blessed by being most handsome,
Most proud of how he could attract the fairer sex,
And claimed himself to be the most romantic one."

"The second spoke in words most complex,
A well-spoken philosopher, a great thinker,
Who said his wisdoms, had gained him great respect."

"A wealthy merchant was the third traveler;
A man whose fortune had grown great from lending,
Whose wealth was unmatched and beyond measure."

"The fourth was skilled in the art of battle strategy;
A mighty general feared by many and held in awe,
Unmatched, was he , in determination and bravery."

"But when the thin veil of Pride does finally fall,
Truth is revealed, and insecurities remain;
For sorrow always comes to those who answer worldly
calls:"

"The Lover, who bragged about the scores he had tamed,
And boasted that his romantic overtures were never denied,
Spoke less proudly, and told about his sadness and shame."

"As though some gentle spirit had touched his mind,
The Lover spoke about the weight of his loneliness,
About the great emptiness he truly felt inside."

"He said he wanted to find true love and happiness,
Wanted to find that one to whom he would wed,
For whom his love would be undying and endless."

"Then he fell silent, and quickly dropped his head.
His face seemed to age, and there was solemn silence,
As his eyes slowly closed as though he were dead."

"The merchant, taken by the lover's candidness,
Was the next to share the truth about his life,
In a voice that was soft and filled with gentleness."

"He explained that his life was truly filled with strife.
'Despite my great wealth, there is emptiness,' he sighed,
'For I know it can neither buy time nor extend life.'"

"He said he watched helplessly as his father died,
As he saw this once great man, this once powerful force,
Become frail as his life was slowly robbed by time."

"The merchant knew wealth could not alter fate's course,
Could not purchase eternal health, love, peace or time.
Then he was silent, lost within his sadness and remorse."

"The general spoke sternly, with confidence and pride.
He said there was not a single thing he didst fear,
Not an army stronger, or a soldier more battle-wise."

"As he spoke about his battles past, it became most clear,
That it was his victories, his ability to make empires fall
And his well-disciplined men that he held so dear."

"When he compared himself to the great Hannibal,
He stopped mid-sentence and became silent;
His eyes and face became suddenly sad and drawn."

"In a softer voice he mumbled, 'Even falls a giant.
That proud Philistine, that mighty great Goliath,
Fell for he fought without Faith and was self-reliant.'"

'No matter how many times I might triumph,
My end is unalterable, and it is certain I will die.'
With sorrow his head and shoulders slumped."

"'No man can ever conquer determined Time;
Persistent and undefeatable, unwilling to be slowed,
Time is the undeniable victor over all mankind.'"

"Silently lost in thought, together all alone,
They each mused about the future, about life's ending,
Until one spoke in a strange unemotional tone."

"The philosopher began, as though lecturing,
Using simple words and a patronizing voice,
He appeared aloof, insensitive, and condescending,"

'Sirs, you fret and worry as though you have a choice.
But, in truth, each one of us is fated to die,
And can only live for those that will come after us.'

'For truly there is no other purpose in life,
But to do our best, to make our mark whilst we can,
And further man's progress in our brief time.'

'I am a great thinker, known throughout many lands,
For giving knowledge and sensibility to the hungry,
For my writing, for my great understanding of man.'

'It has been said that I am the wisest in my country,
I have advised many Lords, Princes, and Kings,
Taught them the power and perils of their sovereignty.'

'Yes, we are captives in Life, unable to be freed.
Forced into a tedious, tiresome play called Time,
To fill a minor role, to exist in but a single scene.'

'But, friends, I share not your sadness in life's design,
But live because I must, so I might learn and share,
So generations to come might learn from my mind.'

'Be like the grasshopper who jumps here and there;
Worry not about life's meaning or things obscure,
Think not about legacies, and live without care.'

"With arms crossed, he said not another word,
But sat smugly with a quirky smile on his face,
Waiting, wanting to argue that Life was absurd."

"'Life is something you should not squander or waste,'
Spoke a mysterious voice from the cooling embers,
'Life is a gift, a blessing filled with Love and Grace.'

'Although by the world you will not be remembered,
You are part of the body of Christ who's loving and just,
Who has a purpose for each organ, for every member.'

'All that's in this world will soon fade and fall to dust,
So, live not for this world, but for the one that is to come,
For treasures stored there will neither rot nor rust.'

'Romantic, place your Love in Him and with His Son,
Love the One who doesn't change and is forever faithful,
Love the Creator, the Giver of Hope, the only True One.'

'Merchant, invest in the One who is merciful,
Work to have a life that is abundant in faith,
Live for Him, and you shall receive Life eternal.'

'General, be victorious over temptation and hate,
For there is none more devious nor more sly,
Than that handsome angel who fatefully fell from Grace.'

'Thinker, this world is filled with deceits and lies,
It cannot be reasoned, it cannot be understood by man.
Truth comes not from without, but from Faith inside.'"

"Frightened, all but one buried his face in the sand,
Wept and prayed for forgiveness and redemption,
Repented, and vowed to live for God not man."

"But the Thinker began to analyze the revelation.
Argued that it was only some odd prank or trick,
Or was some strangely shared hallucination."

"The next day, before they continued on their trip,
Each man prayed for God's strength and guidance,
Prayed for a change in their lives, and how they lived it."

"Before they began their journey to lands distant,
Each promised to meet again the following year.
They vowed to do this, and then parted in silence."

"On the date they had set, three of the men appeared,
Three of them had traveled from their lands afar,
Journeyed to share their story, and the others hear."

"An accident had left the Lover horribly scarred,
But, oddly, he seemed happier than before,
For God's love had healed his troubled heart."

"The merchant, clothed as one now penniless and poor,
Happily told how he had lost everything he owned,
And in its place, he said, he received eternal joy."

"The General smiled, for his story was well known;
All had heard how he had refused to fight rebel peasants,
And how his King was defeated and overthrown."

"Each said that their loss was a blessed present,
A gift that ignited Faith, and made them feel alive;
Amid a dying world, t'was a gift from a living Heaven."

"When it seemed clear the scholar would not arrive,
The men began to wonder what his absence might mean:
Had he forgotten, was he simply busy, or had he died?"

"As the sun began to set, a child was suddenly seen.
As the mysterious figure closer came and neared,
They saw he wore a robe of white, pure and clean."

"When the child spoke, the men were struck with fear:
'Your friend has fallen ill,' the youth said with a sigh,
'And cannot join you this or any other year.'"

"'Sadly, I must tell you that he will surely die.
For that illness, which has fallen upon him,
Has not only taken his health, but also his mind.'"

"Though he is the same without, he is not within;
He is now an idiot who can neither speak nor write.'
The men were silent with sorrow for their friend,"

"Saddened for one whose faith could not be blind,
Who could not understand Faith before his final end,
And had reasoned away his chance for eternal life."

"Come!" said my guide, "There is so much more ahead!"

Lost Leaders

Ere long, we quietly entered a large round room.
Dimly lit was this somber and hollow hall,
Where ornate portraits of men had been entombed.

Standing center, I turned 'round to look at the walls,
'Til, upon one painted image, my eyes did stop,
And I gazed upon he who caused his King to fall.

He led others saying liberty was worth all costs,
But, in truth he was serving Pride and Vanity
And for this, blood was shed and lives were lost.

Guided by growing greed, hate and insanity,
He used his eloquence and guile to ignite a fire,
Not for the people, but for self-idolatry.

But his hopes, founded only on selfish Desires,
Were fabricated with lies, and destined to fall;
Fated to give rise to a fractured and false empire,

Gazing into his painted eyes, I felt his call,
A silent plea to help his cause,to convert,
To share his faith, his belief in Common Law.

I stood staring, my eyes from his I could not divert.
I was his captive, fettered, and unable to move,
Paralyzed by his eloquence, enslaved and allured.

Helplessly, I felt my thoughts being slowly removed,
Replaced, as his soul-less spirit didst mine invade,
As his chilling pursuits did me craftily consume.

Surrounded by a presence I could not evade,
I felt myself move, saw his portrait slowly near,
As his cause I now understood and couldst relate.

"Is it wrong to seek liberty? Why is it feared?"
I cried aloud, though these words were not my own.
Having strayed, I was lost until my guide appeared.

I felt his small hand, as it gently didst mine hold.
As he led me back to the center of the room,
I knew then I could not make this journey alone.

For one cord alone, cannot be as strong as two.
We all need a mentor, a guide, this is evident,
To teach us what they've learned and lived through,

To expose the hidden threats to our covenant,
And help us live a righteous life before God and Man.
For evil, which never rests, is also never hesitant.

Recovered from my stupor, still clutching His hand,
I glanced back at the portrait, now in dimmed light,
Lost amid the shadows, in this self-purposed land.

Another became visible to my searching sight:
He who led the French mob to seek equality,
And sought to amend the commoner's plight through might.

When they were denied their Tennis Court assembly,
Mirabeau returned the King's message without fear,
Stating he would defend his rights offensively.

Directly before us, a large hall suddenly appeared.
Peering into the darkness, on the walls I found,
Silent shadowed figures scurrying far and near.

Each step eerily echoed a desperate sound,
'Til we reached another whom Pride had destined,
Who was the most infamous, the most renowned.

Who believed all means were justified by the end,
That rulers who were feared by people were stronger,
That Trust and Love could a leader only weaken.

Through time his ideas attracted many followers,
Through centuries, he misled with his stealthy lies,
And for this, his portrait was more ornate and larger.

His ideas have defied mortal limits and confines,
Spanned across the ages, by Fear and Pride sustained,
To harden hearts, tarnish souls, and corrupt minds.

Beyond the dark prison, where he was detained,
Through his Princely letter, beyond his demise,
Forever lives his Machiavellian name.

For such men, no thoughts arose, no words did arise,
But my guide spoke the words I could not find:
"Though some with good intention did their plans devise,"

"They became lost as Pride captivated their minds.
Craftily, this new mentor, that now didst them lead,
Altered their motives and their purpose redefined."

"There was once a great gull that flew far out to sea,
Further than e'er before to find his fish,
Though perilous was his journey, he did succeed."

"But Pride o'er came him, and he could not resist,
To fly out again, even further than before;
His good sense clouded amidst Pride's hazy mists."

"Through the clear azure sky he didst glide and soar,
His Pride told him without any help he could succeed,
That he was different, more capable than before."

"That cautions were for others, less able than he.
So he flew 'til land was no longer visible,
And the usual distances didst quite exceed."

"But, when darkness fell, Truth was undeniable,
He was weary and lost, alone without guidance—
Too late, he knew he was fatally fallible."

"Born with a constant desire for self-reliance,
Man forgets God's will and Power does him enthrall.
And, like the gull, he ventures out in defiance,"

"Believing he can deny sinful nature's call.
Created with free will, man has been both cursed and blessed,
And though sufficient to stand, he is free to fall."

"This once great gull never finished his final quest,
But perished drifting amid the vast open sea,
Alone, but for God, in the expanse of darkness."

"In leadership there is a need for humility,
A need to never lose sight from whence we have come,
And be a constant example to the ones we lead."

"Don't be deceived! We are all leaders—everyone.
For though we may not conquer principalities,
We influence and lead neighbors, friends, and loved ones."

"These men created their own dismal destinies,
All, imprisoned forever, without dimension,
Frustrated they cannot further their legacies."

"For what they valued most was earthly ascension,
They forsook their Faith, and allowed Pride to lead their lives,
And for this, they are eternally held in suspension"

"Don't let yourself be enchanted by self-serving lies,
Let Faith, Truth and Love be the lights that lead you,
Follow your Father's words, and let them be your guide."

"For He was there when you fell and when you flew,
He gave you your strength, Hope and inspiration,
So devote time to Him, and you will remain renewed."

"Read His Word, follow His Son, and learn His lessons."
So spake my guide, whose speech didst here abruptly end,
As he quickly turned, not waiting for my questions."

He seemed not to care if he did me offend.
"It is time for us to go, we haven't much time,
Further into Pride's deep lair we must still descend."

Brother Against Brother

We did not venture far into that narrow hall,
Before we saw a strange man sitting on the floor,
Sitting motionless, propped 'gainst a stony wall.

Such a wretched person I had not seen before,
Such odour! Such filth! He was probably diseased;
His body was covered with red blistering sores.

Child-like he sat, with his chin resting upon his knees,
His tangled, long, grey hair concealed his eyes;
With such an unpleasant presence, I felt great unease.

And though I wondered why, and from what he did hide,
I desired naught else, but to leave, to move forward,
And be further distant from his loathsome side.

Time spent with this man, I thought would have no reward,
I was sure speaking with him would be of no use,
For he was surely different than I in all accord:

Different values, desires, perspectives, and views.
"But we are the same!" The man raised his head and spoke,
"Do not let your own Pride conceal the torrid truth."

"For that which you seem to so apparently loathe,
Lies in you, though it is hidden within your heart.
It festers inside, and slowly eats away your soul."

Seemingly exhausted by this cryptic remark,
His chin fell listlessly, and returned to his chest.
My guide broke the eerie silence, "Let us depart."

"But who was that man?" I asked, "Is he possessed?"
"Now is not the time," my guide hastily replied,
Seeming quite anxious to continue on our quest.

"You will know, for in you the answer does lie."
We continued, hastening through the corridor,
That, with each somber step, grew evermore wide.

We traveled not long, ere a light flickered afore,
And I knew soon another lesson would arrive,
And more sorrowful patrons of Pride would come forth.

More men who were fore'er dead, yet fore'er alive.
Damned to reminisce about their lost life and past,
Sadly aware how their heart with wrong treasures lied.

To a damp, dark and dreary room we came at last,
Where a small fire burned amid a fetid pool,
And people sat separated by some social caste,

Huddled, seeking warmth in this room so cold and cruel.
None seemed willing to depart from their chosen group;
All were bound by some certain rite or some odd rule,

Held captive by fear of rejection or rebuke.
My guide explained: "Although they suffer the same fate,
They have traveled very different paths and routes."

"Whether born a peasant, or an honored head of state,
Whatever may be their race, color, or religion,
Each, from their group, were unwilling to separate."

"This was fertile ground for Pride's evil intentions,
To divide our house and pit brother 'gainst brother,
So she sowed the seeds of her subtle deceptions,"

"She nurtured Fear and Mistrust each for the other.
These seeds grew great in some, beyond expectation,
Became rooted in their hearts, and their Reason smothered."

"A shrub erupted to propagate Pride's temptations,
To bear the bitter fruit of judgment, hatred, and spite,
To fill these men with Prideful intoxication."

"And those who taste the fruit, and their juices do imbibe,
Commit such atrocious acts 'gainst their fellow man,
Acts of slavery, murder, war, and genocide."

"Some to prove their dominance, some to conquer land,
Some to show the world that their kind is greatest,
But for what purpose? They are each but grains of sand."

"They blow briefly through this barren desert darkness,
And blend with the terrain when the journey is done.
Though some may fly higher or further than the rest,"

"A common fate awaits and touches everyone . . ."
Just then, a man approached, interrupting my guide.
"Brother! Surely I am the reason you have come!"

"Come join us my brother, come sit by our side!
For the others are nothing but useless heathens,
Wayward and lost, consumed by their own precious Pride."

"They are ignorant, dumb, and devoid of reason.!"
"But why are you among them?" I beseeched the man,
"Are you here to give guidance, to serve, and teach them?"

"To share what you have learned, the things you understand?"
"Of course not!" He replied, angered by my question,
"The very presence of these creatures I cannot stand!"

"Serve these beasts? Surely you jest with this suggestion!"
He smugly smiled and said, "Good man, they should serve
me!"
He paused and said, "Please forgive my indiscretion."

"I didst not intend to be rude or speak harshly.
Truly, it's my frustration that speaks and not my heart.
For I know this is how they were born and bred to be."

That they were destined and fallen from the start;
Cursed to be ignorant, cursed to be led astray.
"Truly, I pity them.," he said before he didst depart.

"Come!" My guide softly said as he led me away,
"There is sadly still something you must know and see,
Come, follow me, for we can no longer delay."

As we walked, an awful stench suffocated me.
As the lake's edge we neared, the odor stronger grew,
The odor of death, rotting flesh, and misery.

And then I saw that which I feared, but somehow knew:
Dozens of dead bodies littering the pool's shore,
The remains of those who hoped Death could Life renew.

"What has happened!?" I didst my solemn guide implore,
"How could they kill themselves? What caused them to lose Hope?
Could they not find the strength to rebuild and restore?"

He answered not, but pointed to a scribbled note,
The final words and thoughts of one lost soul;
His fears captured in the final words he wrote:

"I can no longer pretend, no longer pose,
For I know I shall never be as great as thee,
And though I couldst not change my life, my fate I have chose."

"Now the burden has been lifted, and I am free!"
This man clearly lacked that which would have made him strong—
Faith in our Father, who can make Fear and weakness flee.
Without a word, we solemnly, silently moved on.

A Time and a Season

We ventured further into the depths of unknowns,
Another passage found, another light was sought,
Where Pride woefully echoed her wails and moans,

Where man's earthly achievements counted not.
Where sulphorous smells, most strong and noxious,
Filled the air and for my very senses I fought.

As the rank odor of burning flesh enveloped us,
I suddenly felt my awareness flee from mind;
I felt myself slowly drift into unconsciousness.

Upon waking, I was horrified and aghast to find,
Men on fire, though by the flames unconsumed.
They stood upright, wrapped in flags, all in a line,

Like proud soldiers stoically accepting their doom.
A fate of constant lamentation and searing flesh,
Alone, together, amid this horrid, hopeless room.

Cursed to remain here eternally, without rest,
Forever amid the flickering flames, the noise and smoke.
I desired naught else, than to continue on our quest,

To complete this journey through Pride's home,
And return to my blind, but blissful, ignorance;
To all my misguided beliefs and false hopes,

To a time when I held close to childish innocence.
I awoke from my selfish dreams and desires,
By a desperate voice that had called out to me,

Begging to be heard from within his lonesome pyre.
Though through the flames I could not him see,
I could still hear his painful words from the fire.

"Come hither! Please come hear my pleas!
Please come, and lend me your sympathetic ear!
Do not hasten away, for from Truth you cannot flee."

I reluctantly agreed to listen, and slowly drew near.
"I only wanted what was best for my countrymen,
By conquest, I hoped to free them from their Fear."

"But my insatiable Pride did my good intent upend,
As I caused such misery for the love of our nation,
And no longer, on my Lord's guidance didst depend."

"We believed ourselves to be the masters of his creation,
To be sanctified by his Grace, free from sin and failure.
We believed ourselves to be an army of Christians,"

"Tasked to convert the pagans and them conquer.
In our minds we justified the horrors, and the hate:
We were freeing them from the lives they endured."

"We believed our nation was made strong by our Faith,
We believed ourselves to be like David and the Israelites—
Blessed by God to lead, and chosen to dominate."

"But we lacked Reason, as Pride blurred our sight,
As we misinterpreted and distorted His Holy Word;
Twisted it to make us feel more Just, more Holy, more
Right."

"As His Laws were constantly re-defined and obscured,
We excused our sins as an expression of Freedom,
And allowed immorality to exist, unfettered and unde-
terred."

"As power shifted into the hands of the heathen,
Christian values were viewed as too oppressive.
Too late we learned, even Liberty has a time and a season."

"When Pride is present, Freedom becomes divisive,
And, like children without a Father to guide them,
My people became lost, divided, and self-destructive."

As he spoke I saw the flames abate and descend.
He seemed to understand his past waywardness;
The errors of his life, he did not excuse, conceal or defend.

As we parted, I wondered if his sentence was truly endless,
If redemption couldst be found to free him from this tomb,
If he could be pardoned from this eternal hopelessness.

As we went forth, further into this horrid, dismal room,
I saw thousands more whom Pride had here detained;
Each, in varying degrees, were by the flames consumed.

My young guide then spoke to instruct and explain:
"All were not from nations so 'glorious' and 'great,'
But each allowed their Pride to direct them and reign."

"And, when they forsook the Father, they chose their fate.
It happened gradually, a little more each day,
Compromising their beliefs for the sake of the state."

"With each passing generation, each didst further stray:
They thanked the nation, not God, for being blessed,
And even removed the holiness from their holidays."

"Their society began to further erode and regress.
As children were forbidden to pray in their schools,
And the value of unborn life they tried to assess."

"They felt burdened by Faith, and by God's rules
Believed the church was for the powerless and weak,
That it bred judgment, and did intolerance fuel."

"Any, who's Faith was not kept silent and discreet,
Were said to be odd, strange, and mentally deranged;
Afflicted with a disease that they must cure and defeat."

"Although Christians were derided, abused, and defamed,
Taunted and treated in a most disrespectful manner,
The Church still grew stronger and Faith remained."

"They tried to attack the church with rhetoric and slander,
Fearful that their much cherished power was being lost—
Stolen and assumed by those unified by Christian banners."

"When the Church remained, they enacted unjust laws,
That banned all public expressions and displays of Faith—
They hoped this might stifle the spreading Christian cause."

"When those who were Faithful still defied the laws of state,
They were said to be a danger, a public scourge,
Who must be cast out for all to remain free and safe."

"Their plots to confuse Christians, to weaken the church,
To cause Christ's followers to follow the statesmen,
Failed as the faithful unified, and the denominations
merged."

"For the Lord saw their awesome Faith and blessed them.
He made them strong, despite the State's efforts to sup-
press,
And delivered them from the evil ways of lost men."

"For He is always present, and never shall forsake us."
My guide was interrupted by a strange and eerie sound,
That pierced through the darkness, foreboding and omi-
nous.

Screams echoed, seeming to come from all around,
And though I felt frightened by all that was heard,
In my guide's presence, peace and comfort I found.

Sadly, too many lessons of our youth are unlearned,
As we get older, and Fear does our innocence invade,
It robs us of our Hope, and makes Faith seem absurd.

"We must travel onward," my guide earnestly spake,
"There is much more you still must see to grow.
We must hurry . . . hurry before it is too late!"

"What was that noise, what is that which torments them so?"
I desperately asked, though I knew he would me ignore,
"What is it!? I feel I have the right to know!"

"Onward," he solemnly said, "Onward to Pride's Core."

Battling the Unreasonable

Soon we came to a cold pale place, where a thick darkness loomed,
Where an eerie silence reigned, but for the sounds of distant voices,
Voices that murmured together softly, amid this damp and dismal tomb.

And as we drew near those incessant, those most nonsensical noises,
I grew e'er more curious to see, to learn from what might take shape,
I grew more impatient, to witness man's reward for prideful choices.

But truly, I took no delight in seeing their punishment or their fate.
I felt sorrow for those sordid souls, entrapped in their eternal plight;

And, admittedly, I worried that their fate might me one-day
await.

Aft we passed through a small crevice, hidden to the
room's right,
We cross'd o'er a small stone bridge, which stretched
before us.
But mid-way we halted, at that point which was of greatest
height.

From that height we gazed into the depths below, with
silent solemness,
And looked upon those who nurtured and fed an insatiable
beast within,
Who protected Pride under the cloak of their own Fear and
Weaknesses.

This inner beast grew great, and flourished more with their
every sin.
Within them she bred impish little Worry and ever-growing
Doubt,
To nip away at man's weak Faith, and nibble away his true
Reason.

Relying upon intellect, all Life's challenges they tried to
surmount,
But Faith could not flourish under such analysis and consternation,
And the more they Reasoned, the more Faith was denied
and disallowed.

I saw they were not entirely human, in their insidious incar-
nation,
For in their fallen form, they were now an odd blend of
beast and men,
Each now helplessly transformed, now captive by some
evil incantation.

Some strange spell kept them from seeing the silent serpent
among them,
The monstrous beast that was seemingly amused by her
prattling prey,
But, in truth, she cared not about their musings, but which
would be sent.

Like volumes of moldy, gray and tattered books, the beast's
scales lay,
And her onyx teeth were like countless rows of sharp, poi-
sonous quills.
Her face seemed almost human, though was pale, bloodless
and grey.

Her crimson eyes glowed bright, as though they were
purely evil-filled,
Beacons upon that fearsome face, that possessed neither
nose nor snout,
This I saw, as she proudly poised o'er those she had just
devoured and killed.

The men appeared undaunted by her, and seemed to casu-
ally stand about.
"They are in deliberations," simply stated my innocent
young guide—
Calmly, as though such an irrational reason couldst satisfy
all my doubts.

"Listen, and you may better understand why it is they neither flee nor hide,
How Pride skillfully didst all their good Reason and Sensibility distort;
And has caused them to forsake their Faith, neglect it, and
cast it aside."

"We must not try and kill her!" Loudly protested one
youthful Centaur.
"We should try to understand her, for our knowledge is key
to progress,
And the gods must have some purpose for our pain! Of this
I am sure."

"What purpose could possibly exist?" Lamented one from among the rest.
"What can we possibly learn or gain from our punishment and suffering?
What greatness can we ever achieve, if our very survival is our sole quest?"

"But, it is quite necessary," quoth another. "For without some misery,
Without the Fear that what was accomplished can be lost and removed,
Man will never savor the sweetness of Life, or the greatness of victory."

One said quite proudly, "God cannot exist because He cannot be proved."
"Faith is only for the simpleton—those with little or no common sense.
What we must understand is how Faith has been manipulated and used,"

"For as the Potter, man has shaped Faith to fend away his hopelessness,
To strengthen him 'gainst his Fears, to feel more secure and sanctified.
Man has used myth to mold morality, to craft a purpose for his presence."

"Throughout time, religion has become a panacea for those
weak in mind,
For without a god, to provide structure to the universe, to
guide and lead,
Man's world would rapidly decay—surely, this cannot be
disputed or denied."

"Religion and Faith, are truly the opiates the masses des-
perately doth need,
A sweet narcotic to soothe their ever-present fear of certain
Fate and destiny,
To create a sense of Hope and Purpose where, in truth,
none exists indeed."

So consumed were these men, by their useless intellectual
squabbling,
That their own debate concealed from them the obvious
threat behind,
For as they argued, that once silent beast was now awake
and moving.

They agreed that any plan that was founded on Faith was
of poor design,
And delightfully, into their hearts and souls, crept clever,
crafty Sansfoy.
Suggesting Faith is naught, but an indication of a weak and
servile mind.

Convinced it was most impossible to overpower the beast,
or her destroy,
The men agreed diplomacy was their only Hope to soothe
her or subdue;
And from their troupe, they selected, the most eloquent as
their envoy.

But without Faith in God their plan was incomplete and
fatefully doomed,
For many plans, conceived without Faith, have been fated
by man's Pride.
I cried out to them hoping they might hear me, or might
hear inner Truth.

"You cannot use Reason with such a senseless beast! It is
hopeless to try!"
But upon their deaf ears and stubborn minds all my cautions fell in vain,
And I couldst only pray that their Faith might somehow
awake and arise,

"What is wrong with them?" I asked, "For this man will
surely be slain!"
"Sadly," my guide spoke, "Pride prevents them from
accepting the unseen,
For they reject the One, who can free them from all their
plights and pains."

"For man should not try to understand Faith, in this he
must simply believe.
Watch how this man now proudly attempts to reason with
the unreasonable;
And how he tries, with glib words and artful arguments, to
tame that fiend."

Soon it became very clear how their plan was most foolish
and irrational,
For the beast swept her deadly tail about, and severed the
man at his knees.
And as she stood victorious o'er her prey, who was helpless
and indefensible,

The destined man, now unable to flee, cried, pled and
prayed to be set free.
Though, it was by the gruesome sound of his screams and
breaking bones,
That I learned of his unfortunate fate, the deed itself I did
not wish to see.

When all was quiet again, I chanced to peer upon the pitiful
scene below;
I wanted to witness what carnage might be seen on that
pit's center floor.
I wondered if the tragedy had awakened them, or had broken Pride's hold,

But, the men were again gathered, and their peril was once again ignored.
As their debate resumed, they seemed undaunted by the loss of their friend,
They still could not understand Faith, or believe in the strength of our Lord.

They still did not understand, how God's Grace could possibly save them,
And they clung, e'er more tightly to Reason to resolve their perils and strife,
And they will continue to live within eternal death 'til the veil of Pride is shed.

But those that do receive Him, will receive the glorious gift of eternal Life.
For by Faith captives are delivered, and by Faith the spirit of Hope is re-born.
"Moses delivered the Israelites from Egypt, when he heeded the Lord's advice,"

"And Faith delivered Joseph from his brothers," my guide didst me inform,
And, it was by his Faith, that David did easily defeat that giant Philistine,
And by Faith, that the mighty walls of Jericho crumbled at the sound of a horn."

As my mentor spoke, I noticed his eyes never moved from
that scene,
"Horror upon horrors, that they just cannot see the error of
their ways,
That they cannot understand what a Life without Faith does
truly mean."

When I finally didst see his eyes, I saw his disappointment
and dismay,
His sadness for those souls eternally imprisoned in this
faithless place,
"It is sad how they turn from God, when they try themselves to save,"

"For our strength lies not in hands and minds, but in our
hearts and in our Faith."

A Visit From Poets Past

By the moistness in his innocent eyes,
I saw how it pained him to see Pride arise—
To observe Faith fade, to watch as Hope dies.
But he never seemed angered by these lost souls,
Only remorse for victims of Pride's lies.

Crossing over that cobblestone bridge,
We traveled further inside, deeper within.
Through a maze of rooms, and passages hid.
Lest I become lost in these twisting halls,
I followed closely and placed my trust in Him.

Seemingly, only more darkness was found.
As we wandered deeper and circled 'round
In this most unholy labyrinth underground.
Soon I became engulfed by emptiness—
Unable to see, and deaf to all sound.

I could neither see nor feel my guide,
As the opaque darkness didst all things hide.
And I soon feared he had left me behind,
Abandoned me in this time of great need—
At a time that I needed him by my side.

Why would he leave me to travel alone?
Here in this maze of halls hewn in rough stone—
At a time when such darkness didst unfold?
Did he believe I could find my own way,
In this mysterious maze of unknowns?

As I longed for the light I required,
I felt evermore weary and tired—
Weak from pervasive fears and desires.
Maybe this was why I saw them appear—
Perhaps darkness didst madness inspire.

When my legs felt the weight of an incline,
I wondered how long I had been confined—
For in Pride's house, I had no sense of time.
Hers is such an obscure and vacant domain,
That it confuses both man's heart and mind.

Despite my onerous situation,
I did remain both faithful and patient—
For in this time of trial and tribulation,
I began counting my many blessings,
And was filled with love and adoration.

I was thankful for the gift of sight,
The ability to know dark from light,
For His constant Love that warms me inside.
Most thankful, was I, for His gift of Life,
And for being always close by my side.

So many great blessings have I received:
To be healthy, to be free from disease,
To know love, to grow, to exist, to breathe.
And, for all of these abundant blessings,
He only asks that I have Faith and believe.

When a light through this utter darkness fell,
I felt my Hopes rise, in this Hopeless Hell.
Although from whence it came I could not tell,
I was beckoned by that distant dim light,
That guided me upon those stony shelves.

Clothed in the drab garments of a mourner,
I came upon a man crouched in the corner.
"Welcome to my curs'ed life, foreigner!"
The man spoke, with a strong and lively voice,
That filled the silence of the corridor.

"Carpe Diem! Death will visit us all!
She waits for no one! All are doomed to fall!
Time, she is unkind and she never stalls,
So live your Life for pleasures while you can,
For on you, Fate shall also come to call."

"Give me some wine to quench my burning thirst,
To ease my pain from this infernal curse!
Tell me, was it Pot or Potter that came first?
For I now have answers to these questions,
But how many did I condemn with verse?"

"How many didst I ruin with my words?
How many, away from God, didst I turn,
When I didst glorify sin, and Grace spurn?"
To himself, this poet seemed to ramble,
As though two souls, joined as one, he were.

He spoke again, breaking the brief silence.
In a bitter tone, he said, "Forgiveness!?
Confess I have sinned and seek repentance?
When it was He who permitted my fall!
He who nurtured and fed my faithlessness!"

"I think it is I who shouldst forgive Him!
He made it possible for Adam to sin,
And then cursed us all for his innocence.
He allowed evil to prosper and grow,
And then made us weak to her temptation."

"And now we are all yoked with shame and guilt,
So, my brother, raise a glass to be spilt—
Give some nurturance to our brethren filth!
For nothing remains after life has passed,
But a regret that Life was left unfulfilled."

Filled with his self-indulgent Desires,
I knew here, amid this mirthless mire,
He wouldst remain 'til Truth had transpired.
So I took my leave from this fated man,
And traveled onward, upward and higher.

As the darkness again didst make me blind,
I thought of that lost soul I left behind.
Who, imprisoned by his quizzical mind,
Seeks in vain for a meaning to his life;
But, in this manner, truth he shall not find.

For God has us both cursed and blessed
With the gift of Reason we doth possess,
So we may, our faith, deny or profess.
He allows us to choose whether we will,
Live for this life, or for life after death.

When deeper darkness had deepened fear,
A mysterious image didst appear—
A spectral vapor that drew e'er more near.
A spiritless shadow without substance,
Seemed this essence I couldst see but not hear.

"Whom are ye?" of him I didst inquire.
"I am the one whom you once admired,
Whose words at one time, did you inspire."
The man spoke slowly in a deep clear voice,
Gravely, without passion, without fire.

"For many years I have wandered and roamed,
Imprisoned between these two worlds alone.
Alas! Never have I found my true home,
For one remains dead, and the other unborn—
A Scholarly Gypsy, with no hope of my own."

"When I wandered up to that monkish place,
And saw such peace within that cowled face,
I witnessed the great wonders of Man's Faith,
Yet I thought: 'How many have died in vain,
Trying to change the path of our human race?'

"How sad that man will never change his ways.
He is a wise beast, but an ignorant slave,
That treads in endless swells and rhythmic waves.
For while he lives, he only waits to die—
And is forgotten, once he lies in his grave."

"But we must forgive the folly of man,
For he has no choice, but to build with sand,
In this world—on this unforgiving strand."
The spirit then silently turned away,
And his head fell sorrowfully in his hand.

Before I had a chance to speak to him,
The poetic spectral faded and dimmed.
I wanted to teach what I knew within:
That our treasures should be stored in heaven,
That prideful pursuits are but chasing wind.

There was much I still wanted to relate,
But I knew for him it was now too late
To refill Hope, or change his chosen Fate.
So I traveled on, further up the stair,
Hoping the dark I might soon escape.

Soon the gloom gave way to a shallow light,
And beside me, once again stood my guide.
He never said a word, though from his eyes,
And the manner in which he held my hand,
I knew he had never once left my side.

Deceitful Enchantments

Though I was quite weary, we traveled on.
Winding our way through Pride's many passages,
Until a most beautiful door we came upon.

On the door were seven gold icon images:
A large one on top and six in three rows lower,
Each depicting religious themes and messages.

Some scenes were familiar, some I did not know,
So I asked my young guide for an explanation:
"Here, portrayed in these six smaller icons below,"

"Are different Christian-based denominations.
The largest depicts the One who started them all—
He who transformed the church with his crucifixion."

Then, when he opened the door, such light filled the hall,
To deliver us from our dark imprisonment,
That I was blind, and upon my knees I did fall.

"Raise, and do not kneel before Pride!" spoke my servant.
"For the light you see, is not from a holy sun!
It is a false light—a deceitful enchantment!"

Slowly I arose, and when my eyes did open,
I was shocked to see a beauty I never knew.
Before me was a lush and beautiful garden,

Filled with flowers of every type, color, and bloom.
Vines heavy with clusters of ripe succulent grapes,
Orchards bearing fruit—with each tree perfectly pruned.

Blossoming hedges, groomed into a circle shape,
Surrounded a soothing and beautiful fountain,
Where flowed the clearest water in perfect cascade.

"Let us sit for a moment," I beseeched him,
"Let us partake of this fruit and rest for a while.
Could a brief respite be wrong? Could that be a sin?"

"Stay longer, lost among the errant and vile?"
Curiously he asked, my truest friend and guide.
"Look with thine heart, for this place has been defiled."

"Look, and you shall see, how Truth is concealed by Pride.
Look, and you shall see this is but another room,
You shall see there is neither cloud, sun, nor even sky."

"Come, follow me for time is short, and the end is soon!
Let us follow the path that has been worn by time.
Well-trod by those whose Faith, by Pride, was ruined."

As he led the way, I tried to follow close behind.
I wanted to stray and take some fruit from a tree—
A small taste to satisfy my curious mind.

But his pace provided no opportunity,
And I knew that if I followed my Desires,
I would be lost here alone for eternity.

At a forest, our path faded and expired.
But on into the woods, pathless, we went forward,
Making our way through a web of prickly briars.

Though I maintained Faith in the guidance of my Lord,
I soon worried that we might have wandered astray,
So his encouragement I sought and did implore:

"The path is past, and briars do our progress stay,
How much further? How long must we errantly roam?
I have doubts, I worry that we have lost our way."

"He answered me, "Follow, and the way will be known.
Have Faith and God will provide for your every need.
You won't be lost if you give Him both Heart and Soul."

Suddenly, a man appeared from behind a tree,
"Come, I will lead you to the place you seek and need,
Come, do not worry, place your hand and Faith in me,"

The man spoke with a trusting smile and eyes that gleamed.
He was well-dressed, with rings of gold on either hand;
A respectable, kind and gentle man he seemed.

"What is your name?" I didst, of him, quickly demand.
"How came you to wander in these dismal dark woods?
How came you to live here, within this hopeless land?"

"Your questions," he said, "I would answer if I could,
But truly I know not why I was sentenced here.
Just place your Faith in me . . . trust me if you would."

"Have Faith in my good intentions, and do not fear,
For the ways of these woods to me, have become known.
For here I walk every day, and God's lessons hear."

"Here, in God's temple, I am but a single stone,
The smallest of pieces in our Lord's master plan,"
He said, as his gentle hand was placed in my own.

Frightened, I pulled away from the touch of his hand.
"Please do not touch me!" I said, "For I know you not.
I won't trust and blindly follow a fellow man!"

"How can I know you are not part of Pride's plot?
Maybe you are the evil, artful Archimago—
The deceiver our valiant Red Cross once fought?"

"Where would I be led if I did choose to follow?"
Without a word, the man silently turned to leave;
As though, he had been overcome by great sorrow.

As he left to hide in the shadows of the trees,
I saw how unsteady was his step as he went,
I saw he now used a staff to aide his aged knees.

Cowering, with a back that seemed crooked and bent,
I saw his eyes possessed a strange hate-filled stare—
It was then I knew he had come with ill intent.

His appearance was different—he had long grey hair,
His clothes had changed into a hooded robe of black,
And about his waist, an alms box he didst wear.

Through his fingers I saw a rosary didst sag,
What truths was he trying to conceal and evade?
How did he come to be imprisoned and entrapped?

But ere I could ask, he fled like a beast untamed,
Puzzled, I looked upon the one I trust and know,
The one that understands this world and could explain:

"As we journey to reach our own heavenly goal,
We too will face many trials and tests of Faith—
Like Odysseus, trying to find his way home."

"But we must stay strong until that glorious day,
For the Prince of this world will try and tempt us,
He will try to deceive us and lead us astray."

"We must avoid capture by our one-sightedness,
And becoming trapped in a Cyclopean cave—
For it consumes the desire for righteousness."

"We must sail steadily through life's turbulent waves,
And stay the course between Scylla and Charybdis,
For we are surely lost if we try a different way."

"We must stop our ears when the Sirens call to us,
And be tied to the solid, stable mast of Faith—
Lest we leap headfirst into the sinful abyss."

"And we must be wary of the deceiver's ways—
He will transform us into small ignorant beasts,
For he is only moved by envy, fear and hate."

"And one day, we will be delivered from the sea.
We will find our Ithaka—our only true home,
And then, from pain and judgment, we will be set free. "

"Always be ready, for the time remains unknown.
Be always prepared for the coming of our Lord,
By denying the urge to wander, stray and roam."

Having said this, he walked on and said nothing more.

A Deceitful Shepherd

Trekking through brush, and ducking under thicket,
I followed close behind as he guided our way,
Toward the sound of singing heard in the distance.

I worried not for I knew with him I was safe.
I knew he would always be there to guide me,
And that he would never abandon me or stray.

In times of hardship, when many often run and flee,
He has been there to help me rebuild and restore,
To answer questions and give me the Hope I need.

But, how can I thank Him, how do I Him reward,
For all His Love, His many blessings and His Grace?
Truly, I deserve his condemnation, and nothing more.

Soon we came upon a well-lit and open place,
Where a multitude sang with joy unrestrained—
A festival, it seemed, filled with great joy and praise.

Holding hands, they marched all in the same way,
Circling a fire that seemed to warm the cool night,
Stopping periodically, to cry, lament and pray.

So consumed were they by their well-rehears'ed rite,
That none did cry out to us, or question our intent,
As we drew closer to their fire's warmth and light.

I noticed, as we closer came and nearer went,
A small country church that had been neglected;
Its paint was peeling, the steeple was broken and bent.

The lonely church stood abandoned and rejected,
Its foundation was crumbled, and windows broken;
Time had weathered all, nothing was unaffected.

I listened to the wizened words that were spoken:
"In the beginning, they met together to learn,
Then one arose who believed he had been chosen."

"At first he led their studies of the Holy Word,
But as Pride grew greater within this mortal man,
Further away from our Lord he led them and lured."

"He told the people he was God's newly-born lamb,
That they should place all of their faith and trust in him,
That he would lead them to the new-found Promised
Land."

"He asked them to give money for the pardon of sins,
And told them their Bibles were no longer needed,
Said *he* would define the Word and teach it to them."

"As Pride crept into their hearts and clouded reason,
They judged all others to be unrighteous and wrong,
Abandoned their church, and formed a new religion."

"They praised this new 'savior' in their prayers and songs,
And never thought to question, challenge, or resist,
Because they felt loved, they felt with him they did
belong."

I sensed a powerful presence within our midst,
When I turned to find a man in a robe of white,
Adorned with a gold embroidered miter and lappets.

He spoke softly and calm, without a hint of spite,
"My friends, do you find our gathering curious?
Do you wish to know more, or join us in our fight?"

"We struggle hard together faithfully and furious,
To keep our faith strong and protect one another,
From that which preys upon our mortal weaknesses."

As he spoke, the man didst seem to float and hover,
"In this world without order, and filled with chaos,
We are a family—our faith has made us brothers."

"Here we can live isolated and uninvolved,
Safe from all the world's temptations and dangers,
Safe from those who are sinful . . . the fallen . . . the lost."

"Here they follow me, the one sent by the savior,
The one blessed by the presence of the holy lamb."
So spoke this man, most righteously and self-assured.

I felt compelled to question and challenge his plan:
"But, if you isolate, how can your people grow?
How can they ever reach and save the fallen man?"

"And, is not the sum of many greater than the whole?
Would not the church be stronger if you unified?
Why not set aside differences and join the fold?"

"Are you ashamed of your faith . . . is that why you hide?
What purpose can there be in the judgment of others?
Should not the sinner be forgiven countless times?"

"Were we not told to love thy neighbor as a brother?
Are we not all the same in His eyes and His heart—
Whatever be our sin, our culture, our color?"

He made no effort to respond to my remarks,
Only stood and shook his head condescendingly,
And with a smug smile, he turned and didst depart.

I looked again at the ritual gathering,
Where the sounds of elation had changed suddenly,
Replaced by the chill sounds of fear and screaming.

I watched as they scurried about chaotically,
Some trampling others in their effort to escape,
While others lay prostate, crying hysterically.

Though I looked all about, no threat could I locate,
So I asked my friend to explain their senseless fright,
To show me what it was they wanted to evade.

He spoke not, but with his hand directed my sight,
To where a somnolent and silent lion lay—
A silhouette amid the blackness of the night.

As the people despaired over the end of days,
I noticed that none sought the safety of the church—
They preferred to die, than pass through its rusted gates.

From among the masses no heroes did emerge,
No one came forth to calm them and coordinate—
No one possessed the will, the strength, or the courage.

Each one was selfishly absorbed by his own fate,
And seemingly cared not what befell his brother;
This dividedness only made them weaker prey.

Some were so distraught, and intent not to suffer,
That they cast themselves upon the blazing fire,
Proclaiming it self-martyrdom for the others.

Seemingly disturbed by the now pungent pyre,
The lion arose and took his leave from the stone
And slowly strolled back into the wood and briar.

But, when the king of all beasts left his stonish throne,
And was no longer enshrouded by a veil of darkness,
The truth of his presence could finally be known.

For I saw not a lion of great viciousness,
But a small and most innocent lamb of pure white,
Most gentle he seemed, and filled with great peacefulness.

The people quickly returned to their holy rite,
And despite the lame and the cries of the dying,
The sound of their singing again filled the night.

"Truth will be hidden to those that follow blindly,
For true Faith cannot spring from such shallow waters."
So spoke my wizened guide, after sadly sighing.

"A faithful man who follows the Word of the Father,
Knows he is a sinner who needs to be sanctified,
And knows the way will not be easy—but harder.

"But these men are lost and self-glorified,
They have re-defined the Word to justify their sin,
And have twisted Truth so it is unrecognized."

"The more their ways they rationalize and reason,
The more they do believe themselves to be righteous,
The more they lose direction and their Faith is weakened."

"Truly, His Word is universal and timeless.
It is intended for people of every nation,
A guide to life, to last throughout the ages

A map to guide us to eternal salvation."

Misguided

Aft we left those people to their well-practiced rite,
We traveled on through the wood on a well-worn path;
Somehow finding our way through the blackness of night.

As we walked, I thought of man's present and his past,
How he shapes his own fate, his destiny and fall,
When he does forge his idols—his golden calves.

So many have twisted and re-defined God's law,
Believing righteous acts could save their mortal soul,
And, upon wounded knees, have struggled, climbed and
crawled.

But it is within our hearts that Faith's seeds are sown,
Which, when it's bathed in the genuine light of Love,
Will blossom, bear its sweet fruit, prosper and grow.

Rituals and recited prayers are not enough—
Our heart, soul, and inner spirit must all be filled,
They must be purified, cleansed, and bathed in His blood.

For without the blessed Light, the seeds will be killed.
They will become moldy and rotten at the core,
And will lie useless and fallow amid the filth.

Every Christian is tasked with a challenging chore:
To never cast judgment upon his own brother,
But save him before the Lion of Judah roars.

My mind wandered from one thought to another,
'Til we came to a cottage nestled in the wood;
Seeking rest, food, and the company of others.

As I dined with our host, my guide in shadows stood.
We talked about the mysteries of Life and Death,
Of the ways of the world—the evils and the good.

And all the while a child, who for bed was dressed,
Stood silent in the shadows, and didst there remain,
While I told the others the purpose of my quest.

As I spoke, I hoped with us the child might stay.
But, when I looked to the corner again, he was gone;
"To bed," me thought, "to rest after a day of play."

"He is frightened," spoke my host who was looking on,
"He does not take well to the things that are unknown;
He is shy, and prefers to spend his time alone."

"He has no knowledge of what lies beyond his home,
It is from stories that his world has been defined.
This is how he was raised—this is how he has grown."

"He is a most beautiful child," I replied,
"But imagine, if you will, if you only can,
His being persecuted, killed and crucified."

"For this is the greatness of God's love for man,
That he asked his only Son to die for the world,
Asked him to die so man might hope to live again."

"As Satan was cursed, and from Heaven head-long hurled,
So will be the fate of the fallen on His return;
When the trumpets sound, when His banners are unfurled."

My host, replied, seeming sad and very concerned,
"I know this to be true, and it's why I here live.
For I hate this world, and do all her people spurn."

"For the world has nothing to offer me or give,
It possesses only the anguish of hatred,
And people who can neither forget nor forgive."

Though I so wanted to question what he had said,
I kept my thoughts and questions quietly to myself,
Lest I be cast out with no place to rest my head.

For I could see he selfishly lived for himself,
Greedily hiding his treasure of salvation,
Not wanting to lead the lost from their path to Hell.

And so was the nature of our conversation,
'Til weary, we retired to our rooms at last—
For very soon we would see the sun's ascension.

And as I lay awake, remembering my past,
All my many failures and fallibilities,
I thanked Him for his Love, and for leading me back.

Now, I desire and strive for transparency,
To reveal both my Faith, and my imperfections,
For I know the Tempter's foe is accountability.

Our lives are filled with challenges and temptations,
That can draw us into Sin's stark and dismal lair,
Where Hopes die amid the darkness of depression.

And when the Past brings the pain of Guilt and Despair,
My sore heart is soothed by my Faith in tomorrow,
And by the comfort of knowing I am in His care.

The Sun will shine upon this world again, I know.
It will bring the warmth of Love, the brightness of Hope,
The joy of my re-birth, and the end of my dark sorrow.

This was how my night did pass before I awoke.
And in the morning, ere my travels didst begin,
I yearned to feel the sun, and take a little stroll.

I came upon the child, sitting on a tree limb,
Sheltered in shade, hidden behind a leafy veil,
Protected from the sun's warmth, and the cool wind.

In the light of dawn, the boy didst seem ghastly pale,
With sallow skin and a curly mop of blond hair;
He looked emaciated—sickly, weak, and frail.

When I closer came, I could see how he did stare,
As though keenly watching something distant and far,
As though he ignored my presence or was unaware.

Then, something odd that I did not see from afar,
That I noticed when I drew closer to the lad,
Was his eyes each didst each bear a most frightening scar.

Thinking it was his loss that made him seem so sad,
I asked, "What happened? What took thy sight from thee?"
I know how it feels to lose what you once have had."

"T'was a gift," he didst giggle, "not a tragedy!
My father said the temptations that make us fall,
Will falter and fail if their ways I cannot see."

In shock I stared at him, speechless and appalled.
He smiled, and stared back at me innocently,
Like some enchanted little elf, who sensed my awe.

From his perched position, he slipped down gracefully,
And without a word, he quickly waved good bye,
And ran into the meadow laughing playfully.

When I looked again toward the house, I saw my guide,
"It is time to go," he said, "for soon will come the day,
And there is much you must do while there is yet time."

"His words have been written, His plans have been laid,
And like Noah, there is a task you must complete:
You must build an Ark of Faith if you want to be saved."

"And though some may taunt you, tease and mistreat,
Work hard, follow the measurements in every detail,
And He will supply all the tools and wood you need."

"Many will come to say you will fall and fail
Come to say you're a fanatic, misguided, or dumb,
Come plotting to misguide you, mislead, and derail."

"But, when the task is complete, when the Ark is done,
When you have rescued as many souls as you could,
You will all be spared when the rains of judgment come,"

Then, turning away, he led me into the wood.

Deliverance

As He led me, I felt the warmth of Love,
And could hear a new day coming to Life:
The melodic song of the Morning Dove,
That welcomed the morning star of sunrise,
And awoke the restless bees in their hive,
Saying 'Arise! The darkness has finally passed!
Awake! For the Time has come at last!'

As the warm breeze softly caressed my face,
I could smell the sweet scent of a new day—
The Ambrosic odor of Love and Grace,
That made the Wild Flowers dance and sway,
Like carefree children who run, laugh and play,
So joyous are they, so merry to be alive,
Not worried at all about how or when they'll die.

I couldst taste the beauty all around me,
A sense of peace that filled my heart and mind,
From the serene nectar of her harmony,
Created by Him, and by Him designed,
What other evidence did I need to find?
For the miracle of creation is enough,
To prove His presence and the presence of His Love.

Wading through the meadow without a path,
He led the way with silent solemness,
Until the other side we reached at last.
Here we descended down steep stone stairs,
Into a pit where once the dead were cast.
He led me to an old abandoned catacomb,
Its entrance sealed by a great, unmovable stone.

"It is time," he said, "for me to return,
For us to leave this hollow House of Pride.
For you to live your life as you have learned.
To change your old ways, to cast them aside
So Faith might grow greater, stronger, inside.
Do not become entangled in Pride's wicked web,
But be humble, and by the Light of Faith be led."

"Prepare for the world to persecute you,
They will taunt, tease, and say you are odd,
They will challenge your belief in the Truth.
Hoping you will question your Faith in God—
For this is their plan, this will be their plot.
The ways of the world will only bring misery,
But the way of God brings joy for eternity."

As he spoke, he looked deep into my eyes,
Serious, and with great intensity,
"Always remember, in your troubled times,
That He's always there, if you will believe;
There to bring you comfort, to guide and lead.
Even when you feel most hopeless and all alone,
His Love is still there, and all your needs are known."

"Though His plans are not always evident,
Know he has a purpose and a reason.
Even the Child who was heaven sent,
Had to face the challenge of temptation,
And felt the bitter pangs of rejection.
And, when he was crucified, God's plan questioned he,
Saying, 'My Father, why hast thou forsaken me?'"

"It was for us the Lamb was sacrificed,
Was beaten, abused and hung upon the cross,
To grace us with Love and eternal life,
To save your soul, save the souls of the lost,
And to help build His Church upon solid rock.
He has been Faithful to us, devoted and True,
So be Faithful to Him in all things that you do."

"Know that Faith is essential to your life,
Without Faith, misery lingers, Hopes fade,
Inner peace is lost, and our passions die.
As with Love, Faith in all men is innate.
Though it can never be measured or weighed,
Faith is the substance upon which our Hopes are built,
How lives are made complete, how our Dreams are ful-
filled."

"Live by His teaching and words of wisdom:
Forgive and Love thy neighbor as thyself
Live not for the world, but for his kingdom,
Covet not treasures of worldly wealth,
And live to glorify Him—not yourself.
Love Him with all your heart, your soul, and all your mind,
And the path to eternal happiness you shall find."

My guide then placed his hands upon the stone,
And to my amazement pushed it aside.
From the tomb, a most dazzling light didst glow
A light with the most bright and brilliant shine—
An illumination that purified.
Filled with emotion, I cried and fell to my knees,
For I felt unworthy of His Love I receive.

I remembered my past pursuits of sin,
And felt an overwhelming sense of shame,
For the many times I turned my back to Him,
The times when I denied or cursed His name,
And times I allowed Pride to guide my way.
Ashamed and distraught, I cried out for forgiveness
And a voice replied, "My love for you is endless."

My guide turned to me, and smiling said,
"I love you, and will always be by your side,
Remember Him, and by your Faith be led,
And I shall return when it comes the time,
When it was written, when was prophesied."
Then he turned, and silently walked into the light.
Leaving me watching stunned, speechless, and mystified.

After he disappeared into the light,
The brightness grew great and washed over me
'Til all I could see was the purest white.
And I was bathed in a sea of purity.
I felt my spirit cleansed, my soul set free,
I felt inner peace and lightness of being.
And as I sightlessly spun, I heard angels singing,
Ten thousand voices, with praise and glory ringing.

Then it all abruptly came to an end.
As the light paled, and the singing did cease,
I felt a weight upon my heart again,
I could feel my sorrow slowly increase,
My happiness diminish and decrease.
And though my many burdens were there as before,
I feared not, for Hope had been revived and restored.

With eyes shut, I wanted to hide from life.
I prayed for the return of innocence,
To be delivered from my selfish Pride,
To be freed from Temptation's challenges,
To be blessed with a gift of ignorance.
But my prayers would remain unanswered by Him,
For He knows Faith cannot grow, if not learned from
within.

I awoke from that soporific state,
When I felt a hand gently touch my eyes;
A small hand that caressed my aged face.
With my eyes closed, questions passed though my mind:
Was I home, or still in that House of Pride?
Was the sun setting on my mortal existence,
Or was this the dawning of my deliverance?

The hand gently played with my eyelashes,
It brushed my brow, and wiped my tears away.
It brought comfort, and soothed my sadness,
A touch of love that did my fears allay.
My eyes opened when I heard a voice say:
"Daddy, why are you sleeping out here in the field?
Wake up! I want to play before our evening meal!"

There, looking over me, was my daughter.
With her long reddish hair and bright blue eyes.
Eyes that lovingly looked up to her father,
That only seemed to see the good in life,
And were still unaware of worldly strife.
She silently endured my long embrace
As the sun shined bright upon her beautiful face.

I thought how much I loved my little girl,
As I held her in my endless embrace,
How there is no greater love in this world,
A love that will last until my dieing days,
A love that shall never fade or change.
Then my heart was lifted from sorrow and set free,
For I knew this was the same Love He hath for me.

Hand in hand we did walk home, her and I,
All the while we giggled, skipped and sung,
Happy to be together in this life,
Blessed with a chance to feel and share our love,
To treasure times past, and the times to come.
So, at night, when it was time for our prayers and sleep,
We told the Lord our souls were His to love and keep.

Contact Jeff Morton
or order more copies of this book at

TATE PUBLISHING, LLC

127 East Trade Center Terrace
Mustang, Oklahoma 73064

(888) 361 - 9473

Tate Publishing, LLC

www.tatepublishing.com